The Zed Conspiracy

The Zed Conspiracy

By S.M. Phoenix

Table of Contents

Preface

This book would not have been created if it weren't for the Facebook group Writers Helping Writers and a writing prompt on Reddit from the user u/Professor_Hazel. Thank you for your continued dedication to the r/WritingPrompts subreddit and for allowing writers a safe space to grab ideas.

The prompt: The good news is you've managed to kill the first zombie before the apocalypse could begin! The bad news is you're now on trial for murder…

Parts two and three, however, were created entirely from my imagination, as I wrote part one.

Part one

Zombie Court

"All rise for the honourable Judge Lang", the clerk boomed to the courtroom.

As everyone stood up, as the large door to the left of the judge's bench opened, and the large, burly man, who held my life in his hands, stepped out. Joseph Lang is the only judge in our small town of Fort Kennilton. Having once been highly respected in the judicial community of Calgary, Alberta, after many decades as a criminal defence lawyer, he applied to become a judge in our small town, after the previous judge, Gerald Yuctzy, had disappeared, a decade ago. They say he decided to retire on a beach somewhere, but not even his family has heard from him since he left. Moving his entire family to Fort Kennilton, Judge Lang became one the most important men in this town.

My trial was not like other criminal cases, as there was no jury, which was called a bench trial. I simply had to convince this judge, who knows all the tricks that my lawyer could pull out of his sleeve, that I was innocent.

"Jonathan Bigwell, charged with first degree murder of Allison Tantz, how do you plea?" the Judge asked.

"Not guilty," I replied, my voice holding steady and calm on the surface. Underneath, I was beyond nervous.

This trial was completely ridiculous, if you ask me. Everyone knew Allison, of course, she was well-liked in the community. But she was a zombie, and something had to be done. So I did exactly what you see in popular TV shows and shot her in between the eyes. How can I be charged with murder, if she was already dead?

Now, when I say she was a zombie, I mean exactly what you may be thinking. She didn't just walk, but she dragged her feet like they were both double jointed or broken. Her skin was grey like smoke and her eyes were dull, lifeless. The snarling and wanting to attack me really sold it, though. It was pretty obvious that she was a zombie, which I never believed could even happen.

As I sat beside my lawyer, on the left hand side of the courtroom, I stared straight ahead, at the judge and witness stand. I couldn't bring myself to look at the plaintiff side of the room.

Peter Tantz, Allison's husband, was not only present today, but he was the most renowned lawyer in the city and here to defend his wife. How would I possibly be able to argue against the man who was impacted the most by my actions?

Even though Allison was one of the most respected women in the community, not many people were present in the room, because it was considered a closed trial. Only one reporter was present, as we only had one news station, and only the closest of family and friends. Less than 20 people were in the room, including myself, my lawyer, the judge, the clerk, the bailiff, and Peter. Several witnesses sat in the front row of each side of the courtroom.

While Peter opted for character witnesses both against me and to prove that Allison was the kindest person in the community, my lawyer decided to take a more scientific approach, bringing in psychologists, crime scene detectives, and medical examiners.

"Your first witness, please, Mr. Gordon," the judge said to my lawyer. I had scanned the yellow pages quickly, when I was first arrested and tossed into jail, ripping out the page that listed all the lawyers available in Fort Kennilton. Recognizing Henry Gordon's name, I demanded that he help me fight this absurd charge.

Henry was a short and stocky fellow with balding grey hair and scruffy facial hair. He looked like I pulled him from a dive bar to be here. His suit was very clearly outdated but his methods hopefully wouldn't be. I had confidence in him, even if he didn't have it in himself.

"Your Honor, I call my first witness, Doctor Jessica Vernon," Henry stated clearly to the judge.

Directly behind me, a tall, lanky woman with fuzzy strawberry blonde hair and glasses stood up and walked towards the witness stand. After swearing in, by putting her hand on the bible, and promising to be truthful, she sat down, waiting to be questioned by my lawyer.

"Let's get right to the point, Doctor. Are zombies even possible," he asked her.

"Absolutely, Mr. Gordon. I am a scientist in the field of genealogy and pathology. I have been studying the possibility of zombies for over a decade and have published tons of research to prove my claims," Dr. Vernon spoke confidently.

"Could you give us an idea how that could be possible, in as little medical jargon as possible?"

"Of course. So, basically, we look at zombies as the living dead, or the undead. It has been proven that once a person dies, if they had been exposed to the Zed-Gene, they would in fact turn into zombies. The Zed-Gene, however, is where the medical and science community is stumped - or at least most of us. A scientist somewhere has to know about it, because the Zed-Gene is man-made," the doctor responded matter-of-factly.

"Are you suggesting that someone created the gene to make or control zombies?"

"Unfortunately, that is outside my scope to state, but many different conclusions can be tested, I am sure."

"No further questions, your Honor. Plaintiff is free to cross-examine," Henry walked back over to me and sat down, making notes on his yellow legal pad.

Peter stood up and asked only a single question to the doctor.

"What is the likelihood that my wi - Allison, could have been a zombie," Peter asked.
"First, my condolences to you, Mr. Lantz. Second, this is a better suited question for a medical doctor, however I will state based on my own data and

research, that if the Zed-Gene was present, then it's a clear indication that she was, in fact, a zombie,"

"No further questions, your Honor," Peter sat down, a smirk playing on his lips.

"Mr. Lantz, please call your first witness," the Judge stated.

"Your Honor, I would like to call Dr. Penelope Windhelm to the stand," Mr. Lantz responded.

Upon swearing in, Dr. Windhelm sat at the stand, with her mousy brown hair neatly plaited down her back, and dainty hands folded in her lap.

"Dr. Windhelm, can you please state your credentials?"

"I am a forensic pathologist, which means my job is to run the autopsy on deceased humans and discover the cause of death. This is done through many tests, both physical and biological," she claimed.

"Thank you very much. Could you please tell us what you found when doing Allison's autopsy?"

"At first glance, it was immediately known that she died due to the bullet wound between her eyes," she said in hushed tones. Penelope was excellent at her job, but having to be this blunt with the husband of the deceased made it difficult for her to make her facts sound professional and emotionless.

"Thank you for your time, Doctor," Peter dismissed her, "no further questions, your Honor."

"You may now cross examine," the Judge spoke to my lawyer.

"Good afternoon, Doctor. Could you please tell us about anything odd you found in the autopsy," Henry asked.

"Sure can," Dr. Windhelm glanced through her notes before continuing, "when completing an autopsy it is important that we are thorough, regardless of how obvious the cause of death was, for reasons such as this. When performing the autopsy, I did notice that the brain and body seemed to be in a decaying state. Meaning, the brain looked like it was shot after death. However, the heart showed that it was beating up until the moment of impact. This made any and all other tests inconclusive."

"Can you explain what you mean by that?"

"Well, how can a body seem to be dead before it's actually dead, but the heart was in fact very much alive before it was dead dead? I checked multiple times and even had a co-worker double check everything for me, and came to the same conclusion. I have a report here from Doctor Jasen Alby, who works alongside me as a forensic pathologist, in Calgary," she paused, giving several copies of the report to the bailiff to hand out to the lawyers and judge, "we further decided to run DNA tests and we came across a gene that we hadn't encountered before."

"Did that gene match the Zed-Gene that Doctor Vernon discussed?"

"Well, that's the odd part. We tried matching it to any gene ever discovered, including the Zed-Gene, and this one didn't have any single match, whatsoever."

"What do you think that means?"

"I am unable to give any facts to that question, however, I do believe that it means that someone created another gene but we –"

"Objection speculation," Peter cried out to the judge.

"Overruled," the Judge exclaimed.

"No further questions," Henry said, walking back to his seat.

The doctor had already stated that what she was going to say wouldn't be fact, but Peter had waited to see the response before he objected. I whispered this to my lawyer and he made a note on his legal pad telling me that it doesn't matter. We had gotten the response we wanted, apparently.

Many more witnesses approached the stand, telling the judge how beloved Allison was and that she didn't deserve the end she received. Others came up to try to discredit me as a person, using my past addiction and mental health against me.

I spent over a decade in a constant state of crisis. I had severe depression, which was amplified by my need to drown my sorrows at the bottom of a whiskey bottle. I had lost everything - my wife, my job, my home, and even my dog. What else could I do? Apparently giving into my negative feelings was not the solution, and everyone here today made the judge aware of that fact.

The last witness called was a crime scene detective, who did an excellent job in not making a case for either side. He stated that there were oddly shaped footprints on the ground that appeared to be the result of Allison shuffling her feet. One point for me. However, he said that there was no scuffle of any kind and the bullet entered the body from a point blank position, meaning I was really close when it happened. One point for Peter.

After all was said and done, it was time for the judge to head to his chambers to decide my fate. Thankfully in Canada, I wouldn't die for this, but prison doesn't sound very fun, to be honest.

"I will need some time to sit with all this information, but I will have the verdict shortly," he stated, as he started to gather his notes and the evidence.

The clerk told us all to rise, and when we did, the judge made his way to his chambers.

As we all eagerly awaited the verdict from the judge, I picked at the fingernails on my right hand. The judge, stepping out of his chambers, causing the entire courtroom to rise again, created a hush in the room. The only sound being a dull, quiet scraping sound somewhere in the hallway.

"I have made my decision, and in the case of the first degree murder of Allison Tantz, I find you, Jonathan Bigwell…" the Judge states immediately upon sitting, "guilty."

The courtroom erupted in cheers and shouts unable to contain their happiness. These people were glad to have someone to blame and that person was me.

As the judge started to lift his gavel to bring the courtroom back to order and deliver my sentence, booming knocks sounded from outside the room. Everyone turned to see where the noise was coming from as the door burst open.

Dozens of zombies filled the room, led by the missing Judge Yuctzy. Where did they all come from and how was it possible that no one had ever seen them before now in Fort Kennilton?

There was nowhere for anyone to go, as the undead turned everyone in the room into zombies.

Part Two

Patient Zed

"I can't believe it. It's ready," Tonya whispered to herself, "I did it."

Tonya Farris, an intelligent and beautiful brunette, with bespectacled green eyes, is a geneticist working on a top secret project for the political elite. For three years, she has been working on a new gene, under the watchful eye of the Prime Minister of Canada, Stephen Lemoine.

While Tonya and her team of scientists were kept in the dark about why they were developing the Zed-Gene, she put her blood, sweat, and tears into the project, not only because the job was high paying, but because she felt that she was going to make a difference once she had completed the task set out by Mr. Lemoine.

The only scientist in the lab who seemed to know anything was Dr. Dorian Pearce. He was hired directly by the prime minister as the chief of the project. Everything Tonya did, ran through Dorian. While all the hard work was done by Tonya and her team, Dorian seemed to enjoy taking all the credit.

With a final glance at the microscope, housing the most recent strain of the Zed-Gene, she gasped. She had really done it. This time, however, she wouldn't be going to Dorian. She was going straight to the prime minister.

Tonya raced out of the lab in her black high-heeled pumps, lab tests in hand, toward the elevator. As she waited for it to make its way down to the basement laboratory to pick her up, she contemplated in her head how she was going to share the news.

In the elevator, she decided the best tactic was likely direct, to the point, and as emotionless as possible. The prime minister seemed to appreciate a no-nonsense approach most of the time, if Dorian and the lawyer were any indication.

As she stepped off the elevator, smoothed her skirt, and paced her breathing, she walked toward Mr. Lemoine's office and knocked on the door.

"Enter," came a deep voice from the other side.

Stephen Lemoine was an older man with a thick grey toupee and clean shaved face. He looked even older than he was, probably because of the job. He successfully ran for office in 2006, seven years ago, and has since been in charge of the entire country. Tonya was sure that his job was very stressful and didn't envy him at all.

"What do you want, Miss Farris," he tried to brush her off. He didn't have time for whatever complaint she had about Dr. Pearce. She had come to him over a dozen times in the last three years and each time dismissed her concerns as emotional nonsense.

"Sir, I wanted you to be the first to know," she spoke softly, "I have successfully created the Zed-Gene."

Blinking, the prime minister stared at Tonya in disbelief. He told her to repeat herself.

"Well, sir, the last strain had a few minor kinks that needed to be worked out, and now it's fixed. I have met every single parameter you asked for," she stated, handing him the file folder.

The prime minister held up one finger, read through the lab results, and picked up his phone with his other hand to dial a number that Tonya couldn't see.

"Call a board meeting," Stephen spoke firmly, "immediately." Click.

The meeting room housed a single, large table, in the centre, with file folders sitting in front of each of the twelve chairs.

Stephen Lemoine, heading the table, waited patiently as everyone shuffled in. His board members consisted of his lawyer, Dorian Pearce, a high ranking member of the Centers for Disease Control and Prevention, the head of the Canadian Security Intelligence Service, the head of his newly created Force team, and other government officials. Tonya was not lucky enough to be in the meeting, despite the fact she created the gene.

"Good evening everyone. I know it's late but this just couldn't wait until morning," Stephen said to the men surrounding him, "the Zed-Gene is now ready."

Gasps filled the air as the prime minister told everyone to look at the folder in front of them to see the latest results that Tonya had printed off.

"I need a status report from each of you regarding your tasks," Stephen motioned around the room.

"Recently, I filled out a force team to find and acquire patients to inject the Zed-Gene into," the Chief

Enforcer, Abe Waverly, said, "I managed to create a team of enforcers out of thirty men from different law agencies around Edmonton and Alberta. The best of the best will help us find our patients."

Abe was a tall, dark-skinned man with more muscles than brains. He used to be the head of an entire police department in Ottawa, Ontario, but moved to Edmonton when the prime minister called upon him for his special skill set. A crooked cop, at best, he excelled in making problems, and people, disappear. He didn't have a wife, children, or any family nearby, so he was able to pick up and leave on a moment's notice for the prime minister.

"Well, my job at the CDC is to make sure that the Zed-Gene is used for good, but my role here differs significantly," Oscar Tatton laughed, stirring giggles from the rest of the room, "basically, I am here to keep you all from getting caught, by keeping the CDC off your ass."

Oscar was tall, lanky, and had giant glasses. He was definitely the dorkiest looking member of the board, but he was incredibly smart, which made up for it. They didn't need him to look good, only to keep the prime minister and the board looking good. Oscar's long-time girlfriend, Nina, is a scientist who sometimes helps out in the lab with Tonya, but she didn't have the clearance to be in the room either. Oscar swore an oath to the prime minister that he wouldn't share any secret details with her, and so far, he kept his promise.

"I am still working out the details about what could happen if we were to get caught," the lawyer responded, "but at this stage, I would say that we have all bases covered to ensure nothing comes back on any of the twelve men in this room."

Stephen had decided to acquire the most well known lawyer in all Alberta, Peter Lantz, who was known for being blunt, abrasive, and undefeated. Now that he was the official lawyer for the Zed Project, he was also untouchable. Peter was still fairly young, only in his early thirties, but his reputation made him seem much older. His wife, Allison, is pretty and popular amongst their neighbours in Fort Kennilton, with her bubbly personality and sweet demeanour. Allison is a homemaker but volunteers at the local retirement home.

The rest of the board members went around the room discussing their role, the task they had been assigned, and whether or not they were having success. Every single person at this table was efficient and making progress, if not already completing their assignments.

"At this point, it's time for us to acquire our first patient to inject the new gene into, as quickly and quietly as possible," Stephen said.

Abe had been researching a great number of people over the last six months, trying to determine the best ones to be used as patients. He needed people who likely wouldn't be recognized, had quiet and lonely lives, and could easily disappear without much notice by family or friends. His job was to find people who wouldn't end up on a missing persons poster.

Judge Gerald Yuctzy had just retired and had plans to move to a beach island with his wife. Abe, on the other hand, had other plans.

Along with the entire group of enforcers, Abe watched the judge each and every day for weeks on end. From the moment he left the house until he returned. As soon as Abe had received word about Gerald's retirement, it was time to figure out how missed he would be. Turns out, his wife was secretly seeing another man, and promised to let her husband leave for the island without her.

After receiving the go ahead from the prime minister, it was time to move on the judge. Gerald Yuctzy would become patient zero.

The balding, naked, and wrinkled man screamed as he was fastened to the table with leather straps that secured underneath. No one had told Gerald what was happening, where he was, or why this was happening. Electrodes were secured all over his body - his head, his temples, his chest.

"What are you going to do with me," he demanded loudly.

The enforcers surrounding the table all laughed as Gerald thrashed and squirmed under the restraints. Soiling himself, he cursed and cried.

"I don't deserve this, whatever this is," Gerald's words fell on deaf ears.

After securing the judge to the table, Abe pressed the intercom on the wall and informed the prime minister that everything was set. Immediately, he entered the examination room within the lab, followed closely by Dorian.

Heading straight to the tray beside the patient table, Dorian started opening a package that contained a single-use needle, and started prepping for the injection.

"Gerald Yuctzy, you need to quiet down," Dorian drawled, "screaming and thrashing won't save you."

Gerald's whines became muffled as one of the enforcers stuffed a cloth in his mouth to keep him quiet. His alarming screams were too much of a distraction for everyone in the room to properly do their jobs. This was a defining moment in the Zed project and everyone needed to be at their best. No one could afford to make a mistake today.

"Today, this man becomes patient zero," said Dorian, "and we find out if all of our hard work paid off."

"Patient zero? Don't you mean patient zed," Abe chuckled.

"I like that. Patient Zed," the prime minister smiled, "this is it folks, everyone get in place and let's begin, shall we?"

As everyone shuffled around the room to get the best view of what was to come, Dorian grabbed the syringe, which was glowing with bright green liquid inside of it, and pressed on the plunger slightly, to squirt a bit of the Zed-Gene out, along with trapped air. The injection was ready to be administered.

Using an alcohol wipe, Dorian cleaned a spot on the judges left arm over the deltoid muscle and looked at the prime minister, who nodded at him. Plunging the needle into the cleaned spot on Gerald's arm, he drained it into the muscle. Pressing a cotton swab over the hole, he removed the needle, tossed it on the counter behind him, and everyone waited, silently.

The machines surrounding the patient started whirring, whizzing, and beeping. Something was definitely changing within Gerald's body. While the electroencephalogram showed his brain activity was off the chart, but rapidly decaying, his heart monitor showed his heart beat increasing. Gerald started groaning as every muscle in his body tensed up, causing him to arch off the table.

"I don't think he's going to make it through this," Oscar exclaimed.

"That's the point," Stephen answered.

"It's not supposed to take this long, Sir. The rats and monkeys we used, the change was instant," Dorian offered.

"You know what to do, Abe," the prime minister said, turning to his Chief Enforcer. Abe, who had been clutching his billy club, stepped forward, toward the patient, with a devilish grin on his face.

"Do not damage his brain," Dorian reminded him, "or his heart."

Holding the club high above his head, Abe brought it down with excessive force, right on Gerald's chest. Whack! Over and over, Abe hit the patient, as the room watched in silence. Dorian, monitoring the patient's heart rate, heard the cracking of a bone, as Abe continued to hit him. Finally, after several dozen strikes to the chest, the heart monitor showed a flatline.

The patient was dead.

Everyone flicked their eyes between Dorian, the monitors, and the patient, as no one made a sound. Watching. Waiting.

After a solid five minutes of listening to the monitor continue to flatline, patient zed started making horrifying moaning sounds and everyone jumped. Gerald's skin had started greying and his limbs had gone limp. There was no brain or heart activity on the monitors.

"He's a zombie," Abe whispered.

"Holy shit," the prime minister exclaimed, "we did it."

"Oh my god" Tonya gasped from behind them, causing everyone to whip around to look at the geneticist, who didn't have the clearance level to even be in the room. With her mouth agape, she yelled, "what have you done to him?"

Part Three

Undead Prisoners

The scientist struggled against the ropes that were cutting into her wrists. Being tied to a chair is not how she imagined she would be rewarded by the prime minister for creating his Zed-Gene. Walking into the exam room in the laboratory, that she had spent the last three years of her life in, was the worst choice she could have made.

Tonya Farris was unable to speak, due to the gag in her mouth, but she tried to get the attention of one of the enforcers tasked with guarding her. Wiggling in the chair, making the legs raise and lower quickly, produced enough noise to get her seen. The enforcer looked at her, with an assault rifle held against his chest, ready to put down anyone who dared look at him the wrong way.

"What is your problem, lady," he asked, clearly annoyed that he had to stand there babysitting the scientist, instead of knowing what was happening in the other room.

Tonya had been quickly removed from the lab, manhandled by Abe Waverly, the Chief Enforcer, and thrown into a small room within the basement level of the private building that was being used to apparently create zombies. The room hadn't been used, as far as Tonya knew, for the entire three years she had been there. However, it did smell musty or stale, like it may have been used to store dirty linens.

She asked the guard to remove her gag by pointing to her mouth, hoping he would understand what she was saying. She even added a gesture for please.

Sighing, the enforcer strutted over to the scientist and removed her gag, asking her what she wanted for a second time.

"I need to go to the bathroom," Tonya said, clenching and unclenching her jaw to try and relieve the pain from the too-tight gag.

"Sounds like a personal problem, lady," the enforcer snorted, "you are not leaving that seat, so you can piss yourself, for all I care."

As the enforcer went to place the gag back in Tonya's mouth, with one hand, she craned her neck and bit down hard on his thumb. It did enough damage to instantly draw a large pool of blood into her mouth. Refusing to let go, she swung her head back and forth, hoping to rip the tip of his thumb clean off.

Before she could do any further damage, he used his other hand to bring the rifle down hard on the top of her head, causing her to black out.

A massive headache and blurry vision is all Tonya could feel when she came to. Disoriented, she could still taste the blood in her mouth. The gag had been removed, but her tongue felt heavy and dry.

"Good morning sunshine," a deep voice had said to her, chuckling to himself. It was Dorian Pearce.

Looking around, the scientist realised that she was still in the same room as before, only this time, she was covered in her own urine and blood. Starting to acclimate to her environment, her own stench made her want to vomit.

"Why are you all doing this to me," she questioned.

"You will have to wait for the prime minister for that answer," he responded, leaning casually on the wall furthest away from her.

As if his ears had been burning, Stephen Lemoine entered the room, followed closely by Abe, who motioned for his enforcer to leave the room, which he did in a huff.

"Hello Tonya," Stephen said, as another enforcer quickly brought in a chair for the prime minister to sit in, and left again.

"Why are you doing this to me," she demanded again.

"I think the better question would be what is happening here, don't you think," the prime minister offered. With Tonya's eyes fixed on him, he continued, "you created the perfect gene mutation to create zombies. That's what is happening here."

"But why? What is the point in making zombies," she asked.

"Simple. Population control and to establish confidence in my government so I can stay in rule longer," he said as if it was obvious and she lacked common sense, "I know, it sounds weird to kill people just to turn them into zombies, but it makes sense if you think about it. We kill off a few people, okay, maybe more than a few, and then we dump them at random, to kill off people at random. They may end up dead, like we hope, but there is also the possibility that a zombie gets killed."

"Let me guess, that benefits you somehow too," Tonya spit as she bit the words out.

"Of course. A zombie gets killed, and we can set the person up for a murder charge, and put them in prison. No one is going to believe that they killed a zombie, they will be seen as a murderer and likely crazy," Stephen looked pleased with himself, like he thought of everything that could possibly go wrong, "we have already began replacing judges, officers, and more with people who belong to the Zed Project, including the judge that will take over for Gerald."

"I can't believe you are doing this. Someone will find out. Think about this logically, Sir, the world won't look the other way. Someone here will tell," she tried to negotiate with the prime minister, though she figured it wouldn't work.

"That's where you're wrong," Stephen stated, "there is no one here that knows what we are doing."

Realizing his meaning, Tonya started praying and crying. She begged for the prime minister to change his mind.

"I'm sorry, Tonya," the prime minister said, clearly not sorry in the least, "you know too much."

One of the enforcers pulled out his pistol and shot the scientist point blank in the chest. Being hooked up to monitors told them immediately that he had missed her heart, yet managed to kill her instantly.

Testing his curiosity, Dorian injected the Zed-Gene into Tonya's lifeless arm. He wanted to know what would happen if it was given after the body was already dead.

Staring at the monitors, Dorian watched as Tonya instantly started decaying and turning into a zombie.

"Looks like you can kill them before injecting them," Dorian said casually as the prime minister clapped.

"We need more patients, Abe," Stephen said in the middle of the meeting room once more, as the board debriefed the situation, "Gerald and Tonya are not enough. I thought you had been researching all these people to use?"

"I did! You didn't tell me that you wanted them all here at the lab right away," the Chief Enforcer yelled, "we will go get them right now, Sir!"

"Watch your tone boy, or you'll be getting the injection next," Dorian growled, "that's still the prime minister and you are a nobody."

"Stop fighting," James Poltin commanded, "I have an idea."

Everyone went back to their seats, glaring at each other, hoping that what the head of the Canadian Security Intelligence Service, James, would say could solve their issues.

"Listen, Abe could easily run out and find new patients, but what if we tried something new?"

"New how? What do you have in mind, Jimmy," Oscar asked his long time friend.

"Well, why don't we just look closer to home, like prisoners, or people about to be prisoners, or the homeless population?"

Shooting out of his seat with such force that the chair flew back against the wall, Peter, the lawyer, had an even better idea.

"That's a great idea, but I can do one better," he said grinning, "Thinking close to home, I'd like to offer up my wife Allison to be injected."

In the basement of the building, a long hallway was lined with cells that looked like they belonged in a prison. Each and every barred room housed a zombie. The judge, Tonya, some of the homeless population, and several prisoners had all been turned into zombies and locked up tight.

Allison, however, who had been injected immediately following the board meeting, after her husband, Peter had convinced her to come with him to work, was nowhere to be found. Peter had been granted special permission to take her home with him, as long as she wore a shock collar attached to a rubber leash and a straight-jacket. He kept her locked up in their bedroom, where she struggled against the restrictions while he slept soundly in their bed.

A few weeks after the last patient, Allison, had been turned, Peter woke up and followed his usual morning routine. Walking straight to the bathroom, he urinated, brushed his teeth, and had a shower. When he came back to the room to get dressed, he realized that something was missing - or someone. Allison wasn't attached to the leash.

Walking over to where she was secured, Peter immediately noticed the jagged end of the leash. Allison had chewed her way out of the restraint. With her shock collar and straight-jacket still on, she managed to escape the house without harming a single hair on Peter's head.

Grabbing the remote to her collar, he ran outside after dressing himself, smashing his thumb on the button to initiate an electric shock in her collar, hoping she would be close enough to feel it. He searched for over an hour, calling her name, unsure if she would even know it anymore.

She was gone, but he wouldn't stop searching for her.

A man was walking down a back alley behind a tacky restaurant, on his way back to his apartment, when he heard the sounds.

Strange shuffling noises, coupled with growls and moans, came from somewhere ahead of him. He continued cautiously, as he put one hand on the pistol that he carried inside the back of his pants.

Just then, a woman appeared, with her limbs loose at her side, scraping her feet against the ground, groaning, as she inched closer to the man. Growling, she lunged for him as soon as she was within arms reach. The man dove backwards to get away from what appeared to be a decaying woman, but she kept coming at him.

Behind the scuffle, Peter rounded the corner, after catching up with his wife. Seeing the situation in front of him, he ducked behind a garbage can to watch the entanglement, and phoned the police.

As the undead woman kept clawing at the man, he reached into the back of his pants, and pulled out his pistol. He yelled at the woman to back off, but she didn't listen. He had no choice.

BANG!

The man had shot the woman directly between the eyes causing her to crumple to the ground. As the man sat, out of breath, he heard sirens in the distance. Wondering what the hell he just encountered, he shook from head to toe, still in shock of the assault. He'd watched a great number of tv shows and he knew what a zombie was, but could they possibly be real?

As the police cars coming at him stopped, the officers immediately jumped out, pointing their guns at the man, telling him to stand up. He threw his hands up and tossed the gun to his side.

"I was just attacked and used my gun in self defence, she's over there, but something is wrong with her," he yelled desperately.

As the police officers moved in closer, one of them came forward and grabbed the man by the wrists, spun him around, and slapped a set of handcuffs on him. Another, reached inside the man's pants and pulled out his wallet.

Peter jumped out from behind the garbage can, running toward the police, waving his hands.

"That's my wife! He killed my wife," Peter screamed. One of the officers put an arm out and caught Peter before he could get closer to the scene.

"Jonathan Bigwell, you are under arrest for the murder of Allison Tantz."

Acknowledgements

To my children, who sacrifice quantity time with me, so I can write (which we make up for with quality time). Khloe and Charlee, you little ladies are my entire world, and the reason why I pursue my goals. I want to show you that dreams really come true, and they have for me since the day each of you were born.

To my dog, Ollie, who encourages me to take breaks from my project, with his gentle elbow biting, laying on my laptop, and pacing because he needs to go to the bathroom.

To my boyfriend, Chris, who not only helps hold down the fort when I get into the writing zone, but for being a sounding board when I get stuck in my own head.

To the amazing Facebook and Reddit spaces for writers, without you all, this short story collection would have never been created, let alone published.

To my friends, who always encourage me to write more, and constantly tell me how good I am - I may not believe you, but it does help me type more words per day.

About The Author

S.M. Phoenix is the fantasy and science fiction pen name for author Shannon L. McIntyre.

Shannon is a full time university student and mother of two daughters and a Great Dane named Ollivander (Ollie).

Reading and writing for as long as she can remember, Shannon is an avid novel and notebook collector. As a self-proclaimed nerd, she takes part in many fandoms. Shannon is obsessed with exotic birds, specifically flamingos, ostriches, and peacocks, the colour rose gold, true crime, and board games.

Known as a tumbleweed who never stays in the same place for long, she is currently settled in the Waterloo Region, in Ontario, Canada, until the next strong wind takes her away. Her dream is to move out East.

If you are interested in learning about the other pen names she writes under, you can follow SLM Publishing on Facebook and Instagram at @SLMPublishing.

Free Digital Download

Scan this QR code to fill out a form for your FREE digital download of The Zed Conspiracy, as a thank you for purchasing my novel.

Printed in Great Britain
by Amazon